BLACKBERRY FARM

MRS SQUIRREL AND HAZEL

Jane Pilgrim

This edition first published in the United Kingdom in 2000 by
Brockhampton Press
20 Bloomsbury Street
London WC1B 3QA
a member of the Caxton Publishing Group

Reprint 2002

Designed and Produced for Brockhampton Press by
Open Door Limited
Rutland, UK

Illustrator: F. Stocks May
Colour separation: GA Graphics Stamford

Title: BLACKBERRY FARM, Mrs Squirrel and Hazel
ISBN: 1-84186-044-1

Printed in Singapore by Star Standard Industries Pte. Ltd.

MRS SQUIRREL AND HAZEL

Jane Pilgrim

Illustrated by F. Stocks May

BROCKHAMPTON PRESS

Mrs Squirrel lived with her daughter Hazel in a large oak-tree down the lane past Blackberry Farm. In the summer they played amongst the big branches, and in the winter they kept warm inside their house in the big tree trunk.

Hazel was a very pretty little
squirrel with a large fluffy tail,
and she was very fond of pretty
dresses. Mrs Squirrel liked her
best in green ones.

One day Hazel said to her mummy: "Please, Mummy, may I have a new frock? My green one is getting very tight for me, and please could I have a blue one?"

Now Mrs Squirrel was a very busy person, because she kept their little house in the tree very clean and tidy, and was always sweeping and dusting and polishing. And when she was not doing that she was busy collecting nuts for their winter store. "You will have to wait, darling," she said, "Mummy is too busy to make you a new dress now." And she went on with the polishing.

Hazel was very sad and sat down on one of the big branches of the oak-tree and dropped a few large tears down the front of her old green dress.

Just then Joe Robin came flying past, he saw little Hazel looking very sad and stopped to ask her what was wrong. "I want a new frock, Joe Robin," she sobbed. "And my mummy is too busy to make me one, and this old green one is getting too tight for me." And a few more tears rolled down the front of her old green dress.

Joe Robin felt very sorry for her and he thought very hard for a few minutes. "Cheer up, Hazel," he chirped, "I believe Lucy Mouse would make you a dress. She is a very good stitcher. I will tell your mummy." And he called out cheerfully to Mrs Squirrel: "Can I speak to you for a minute, Mrs Squirrel?"

Mrs Squirrel was delighted. "Thank you very much, Joe Robin," she said. "It would be a great help to me. I will go and see her at once. Dry your tears, Hazel darling. You shall have a new dress if Lucy Mouse can make it for you, and it shall be a blue one with a white frilly collar and a large white sash." And off they went to find Lucy Mouse.

Lucy Mouse was at home in one
of the stables at Blackberry Farm.
She listened carefully to all that
Mrs Squirrel said. then she got out
her tape-measure and carefully
measured little Hazel, so that she
could make the dress the right
size. "Come and see me again in
three days' time," she said. And
they thanked her very much and
went happily back to their oak-tree.

And Lucy Mouse got out of her
cupboard a large roll of blue stuff,
a large pair of scissors, and a
packet of pins. Then she fetched
her needle and cotton and began
to work.

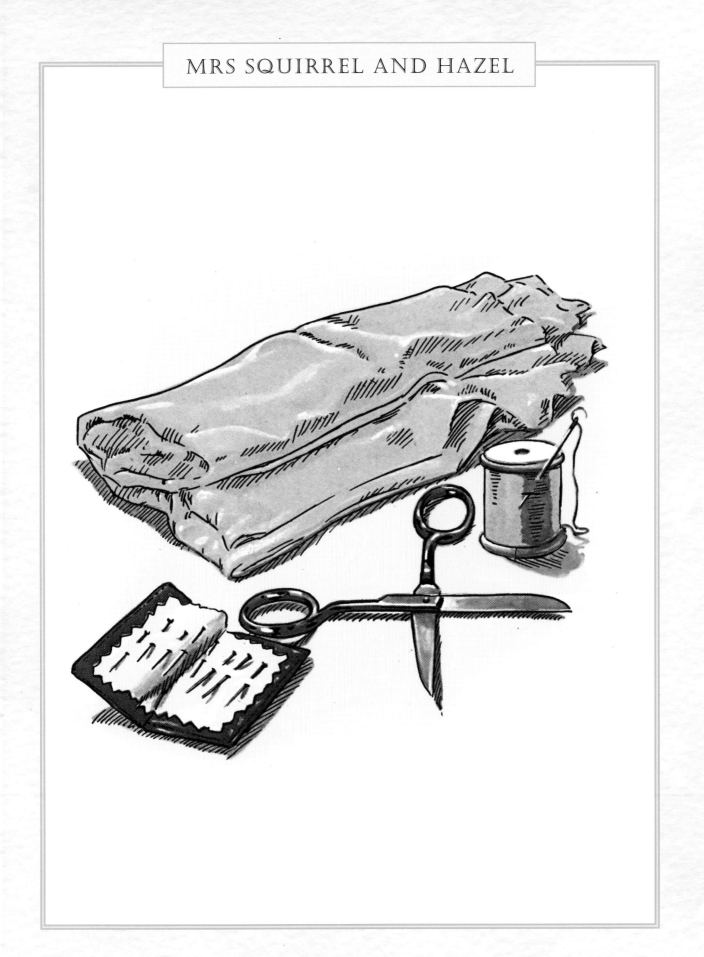

Three days later Mrs Squirrel
and Hazel went back to see Lucy
Mouse. They waited anxiously for
her to open the door. Would the
dress be ready?

MRS SQUIRREL AND HAZEL

It was ready. And it was quite the most beautiful dress that Mrs Squirrel and Hazel had ever seen. It was blue, and it had a white frilly collar, and a large white sash, and a lovely, lovely sticking-out skirt.

Hazel was so happy that she
kissed and hugged Lucy Mouse.
"Thank you," she cried. "It is the
prettiest frock I have ever seen."
And Mrs Squirrel said: "Thank
you, Lucy Mouse, very, very much.
You have been a great help to me."
And Lucy Mouse said: "Now Hazel
must try it on."

So Hazel tried it on, and it was just the right size. She stood up on the table and danced for joy, and Mrs Squirrel told Lucy Mouse that she thought it was the prettiest frock she had ever seen. Then Lucy Mouse packed it up carefully in a large cardboard box, and they all went back to tea in the big oak-tree down the lane past Blackberry Farm.